Moose's Loose Tooth

by Jacqueline A. Clarke
Illustrated by Bruce McNally

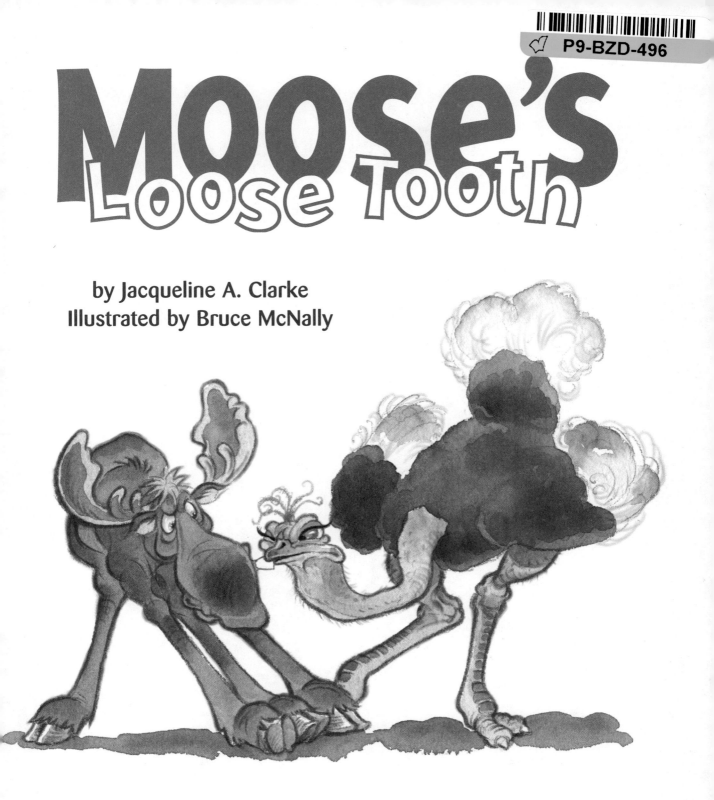

SCHOLASTIC INC.
New York   Toronto   London   Auckland   Sydney
Mexico City   New Delhi   Hong Kong   Buenos Aires

For Garrett, may the tooth fairy treat you well!
— J.A.C.

For Frances, with love
— B.M.

ISBN 0-439-41183-1

Text copyright © 2003 by Jacqueline A. Clarke.
Illustrations copyright © 2003 by Bruce McNally.
All rights reserved. Published by Scholastic Inc. SCHOLASTIC and associated logos are trademarks and/or registered trademarks of Scholastic Inc.

12 11 10 9 8 7 6 5   4 5 6 7 8/0

Printed in the U.S.A. • First printing, February 2003 • Book design by Nathan Gassman

Moose walked into a tree and bumped his tooth. "Ouch!" he cried. "These big teeth of mine are always getting in the way."

He felt his tooth with his tongue. "My tooth is loose," he said. "It's a wibbly, wobbly tooth! When it falls out, I can put it under my pillow for the Tooth Fairy. I'll bet she's never seen a moose's tooth before."

Several days passed, and Moose's tooth was still wibbly, wobbly.

He was tired of waiting for it to fall out.

Just then, Bird came by. "Tooth trouble, eh?" asked Bird.
"Let me help."

Bird grabbed onto Moose's tooth with his beak. He pulled with all his might, but that tooth just held on tight.

"Stubborn tooth," said Bird.

Just then, Tiger came by. "Tooth trouble, eh?" asked Tiger.
"Let me help."

Tiger pulled Bird. Bird pulled the tooth – the wibbly, wobbly tooth.
They pulled with all their might, but that tooth just held on tight.

"Stubborn tooth," said Tiger.

Just then, Zebra came by.
"Tooth trouble, eh?" asked
Zebra. "Let me help."

Zebra pulled Tiger. Tiger pulled Bird. Bird pulled the tooth — the wibbly, wobbly tooth. They pulled with all their might, but that tooth just held on tight.

"Stubborn tooth," said Zebra.

Just then, Giraffe came by.

"Tooth trouble, eh?" asked Giraffe. "Let me help." Giraffe pulled Zebra.
Zebra pulled Tiger. Tiger pulled Bird. Bird pulled the tooth – the wibbly,
wobbly tooth. They pulled with all their might, but that tooth just held
on tight.

"Stubborn tooth," said Giraffe.

Just then, Elephant came by.

"Tooth trouble, eh?" asked Elephant. "Let me help."
Elephant pulled Giraffe.

Giraffe pulled Zebra. Zebra pulled Tiger. Tiger pulled Bird.
Bird pulled the tooth – the wibbly, wobbly tooth.

They pulled with all their might, and FINALLY that tooth took flight!
It flew past Bird. It flew past Tiger. It flew past Zebra. It flew past Giraff
And it flew right into Elephant's mouth. Gulp!

"Now what can we do?" asked Moose. Moose looked at Bird. Bird looked at Tiger. Tiger looked at Zebra. Zebra looked at Giraffe. Giraffe looked at Elephant.

"You can have one of my tusks," said Elephant.

"No, thank you," said Moose. "The Tooth Fairy wants to see a moose's tooth. You're coming with me, Elephant!"

So Moose (with a little help from Bird, Tiger, Zebra, and Giraffe) picked up Elephant and carried him to Moose's bed.

"You're sleeping here tonight," said Moose as he shoved Elephant under his pillow.

The next morning, after a bumpy night's sleep, Moose woke up.

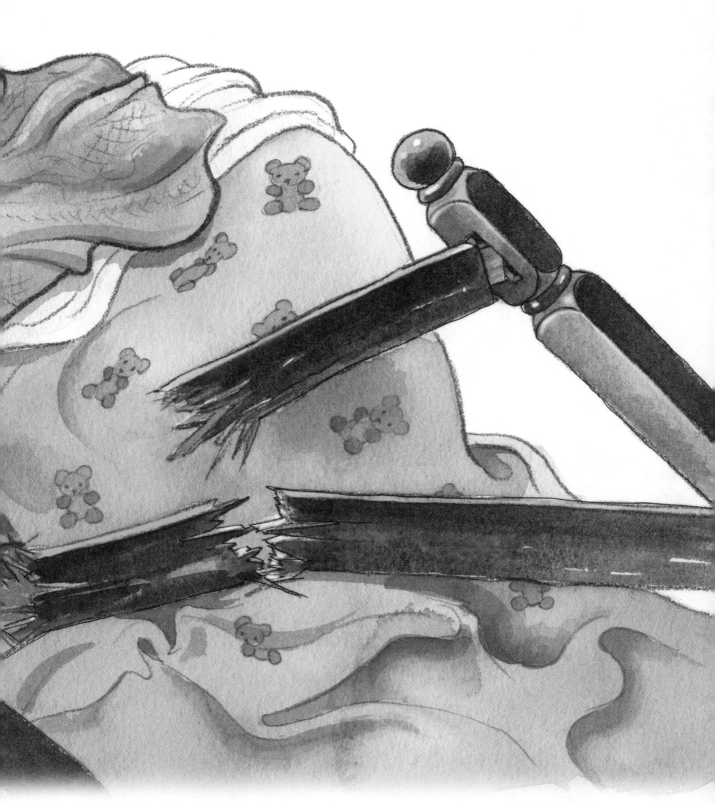

He lifted his pillow and found Elephant still sound asleep.

"Wake up, Elephant," said Moose. "We need to see if the Tooth Fairy came."

Elephant moved out from underneath the pillow. Where he had slept were five shiny quarters – one for Moose, one for Bird, one for Tiger, one for Zebra, and one for Giraffe.

"Where's my quarter?" asked Elephant. "Did the Tooth Fairy forget me?" Moose and Elephant lifted the pillow once again.

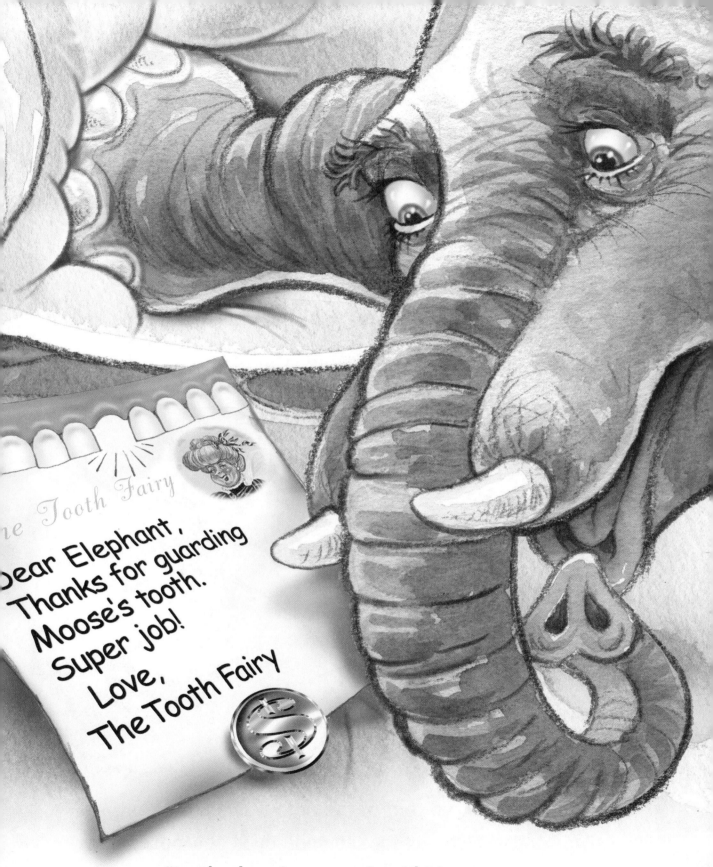

"Look, there's a note," said Moose.

The Tooth Fairy

Dear Elephant,
Thanks for guarding
Moose's tooth.
Super job!
Love,
The Tooth Fairy

Attached to the bottom of the note was a shiny
silver dollar. Elephant looked wide-eyed at Moose.
Moose looked wide-eyed at Elephant.

"Wow, so that's what happens when the Tooth Fairy visits,"
said Moose.

"I think I have a loose tusk," said Elephant.
And together they went to find Bird.